SO SMALL

WEEKLY READER BOOK CLUB

PRESENTS

So Small

BY ANN RAND

WITH PICTURES BY FEODOR ROJANKOVSKY

HARCOURT, BRACE & WORLD, INC., NEW YORK

by Ann Rand and Feodor Rojankovsky
THE LITTLE RIVER

by Ann and Paul Rand
I KNOW A LOT OF THINGS
SPARKLE AND SPIN
LITTLE 1

by Ann Rand and Olle Eksell
EDWARD AND THE HORSE

WEEKLY READER BOOK CLUB EDITION

To Catherine, Leyla,

and Ayshe

Once a mother and father mouse
who lived in the wall
of a nice country house
had a litter of six little mice.

Five were the size
that mice should be,
but the sixth was so small
that it was hard to realize
he was a mouse at all.

"He's just eyes and ears!"
cried the father.
"He has hardly any tail,"
wailed the mother.

The five grew and grew;
the sixth did too
but such a little
there still wasn't much
mouse to see.

"We have to admit
he will always be small."
The parents sighed
and decided to call him
Little Bit.

Now the five were very good
and always behaved as they should.
They stayed near home and played
and were glad
with whatever they had
for supper.
But Little Bit
had already begun to sit
and think of naughty things to do.

"Your father wants to speak to you,"
the mother said one day.
"And most of all to Little Bit
because he is so small."

"Now the world of a mouse
is very hard,"
the father sternly said.

PUSSYCAT

OWLS

"We only get the crumbs of bread;
we must watch out
for traps and brooms and owls
or taking naps
wherever pussycats may prowl."
"We will take care," said the five,
but Little Bit,
who was very nimble,
decided to dive inside a thimble,
and no one was sure he even heard
his father's warning word.

Probably not
because the very next day
when it was hot,
Little Bit went out to sleep
in the shadow of a clover leaf,
and woke from a lovely dream
of peanuts, cake,
and green ice cream
when a big cat howled in glee,
"What is this tiny thing I see!"

Little Bit,
who was very proud,
shouted: "I'm a mouse,
not a thing!" so loud
that the cat scurried back
to the house.

But at night when Little Bit
came home to boast,
he only got dry toast
for supper.
"I may be small," thought Little Bit,
"but I'll show them all!
It's better to be brave
than never misbehave."

Early next morning
mother mouse gave warning
to keep away from the cook,
but Little Bit
just had to have a look.

And as soon as he was able,
he sneaked out and climbed
the kitchen table;
only the cook
was nowhere to be found
when Little Bit peeped around.

He was about to go
when he knocked over a cup
that was full to the brim
and decided instead
to go for a swim
in a pool of milk,
and then thought what fun
to leap onto this heap of flour,
but the flour stuck like glue
as flour will do with milk.

Poor Little Bit,
he nearly had a fit of terror.
He kicked his tiny feet
and beat his tiny paws,
but all he did was roll and roll
till he grew as big
as a mixing bowl.

He looked like a live ball of batter
to the cook who came crying:
"Whatever's the matter
with the cake I was going to make!"

"Oh dear," thought Little Bit,
"I don't want to be baked!"
So he kicked and flounced
and bounced so hard that
the cook screamed with fright
and to Little Bit's delight
ran away.

Little Bit stopped kicking his feet
and began to eat
so fast that at last
he got out and hid
in a laundry sack
before the cook came back
to the room
waving a big yellow broom.

That night mother mouse
said she hadn't known
how fat her Little Bit had grown.
Little Bit was glad
for once he wasn't small,
but he didn't like at all
the medicine he had to take
to cure his stomach ache.
Even so, that night in bed
he thought what fun
it was to do as he had done,
and how it was still better
to be brave
than never misbehave.

Every day when Little Bit played
with his sisters and brothers,
each one tried to do more
than the others.
They raced up walls
and curled into balls
to roll down the cellar stairs.

"I can do most," boasted Little Bit.
"I can climb a daisy
like a tree, you see."
"But so can we," laughed the five.
"I can hop a raindrop,"
Little Bit said.
"But we can jump six in a row
and know how to leap
a pile of sticks," teased the five.

"So can I!" cried Little Bit.
But when he tried, he found
the pile was much too high.

"Poor Little Bit," said the five.
"There are lots of things
you can never do
because you are too small."

This made Little Bit so cross that
he tossed his tiny head and said :
"I may be small,
but I'm braver than you all.
I'm not afraid of a cook
with a broom
or a prowling cat,
and even more than that
I'm not afraid of an owl!"

Before the five could reply
or even say good-by,
Little Bit ran as fast as he could
into a big dark wood.

Inside the forest
it was almost like night,
and Little Bit
nearly swooned with fright
when he bumped plunk!
into the trunk of a tree
and saw an upside-down stump
hump up like the head of a ram.
"Oh dear," moaned Little Bit aloud.
"I mustn't forget how brave I am."

"Whooo whooo are you
to be so brave?" cooed a voice
so close to his ear
that Little Bit leaped
right off the ground in fear.
"A frog perhaps,"
said the owl, peering closer.
"Or maybe a miniature dog?"
Poor Little Bit,
he couldn't say a thing
or even bring himself to look
at those two enormous eyes.

"Why it's a mouse," said the owl,
pretending to be surprised.
"Just step up here, my dear,
and I'll give you something
to make you wise."
But Little Bit knew
that this was a trick
and he had to do something quick
or
there wouldn't be a Little Bit
any more.

Just then he spied
an empty acorn shell.
Like a flash
he dashed inside to hide,
and the owl,
who couldn't see very well,
was awfully mad
because he couldn't tell
where Little Bit had gone.
"Where are you, pray?" coaxed the owl.
"I'm always very nice to mice."
But Little Bit didn't stay
to listen.
He just quietly rolled away.
And he decided as he rolled
it was fine to be bold and brave
but sometimes better to do
as you're told
and not always misbehave.

(But most of all, Little Bit
was very glad
that he was small enough to fit
an acorn shell.)